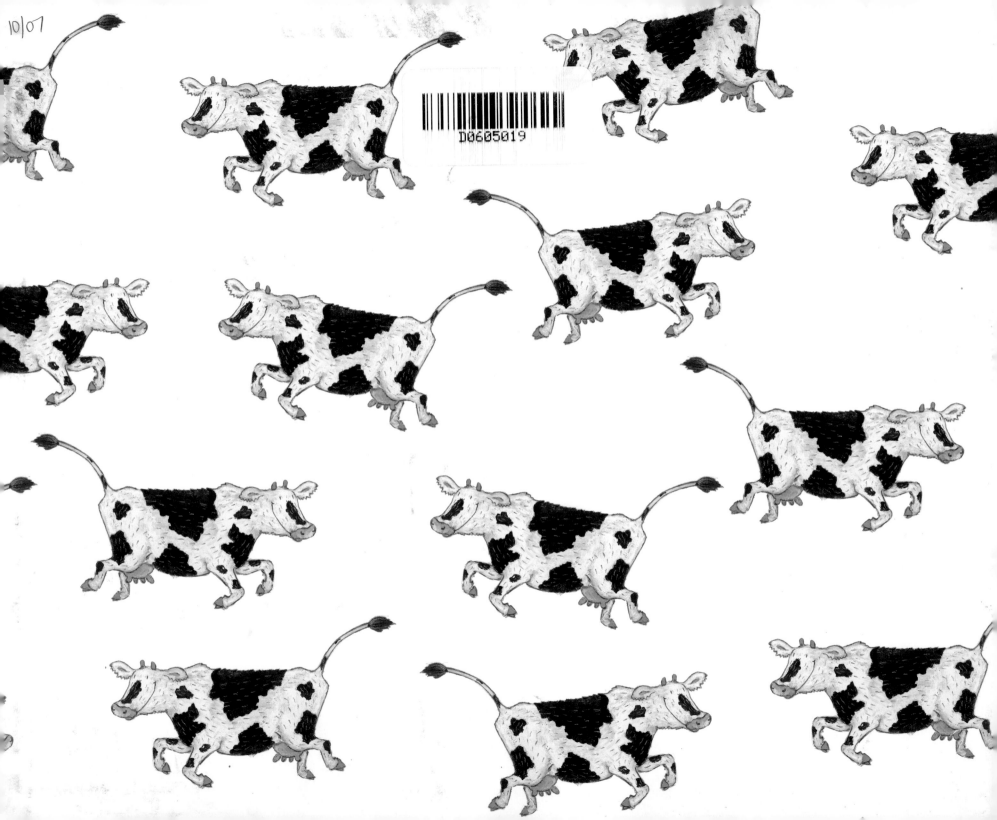

Gloria the Cow

By Paul Maar

Illustrated by Tina Schulte

Translated by Alexis L. Spry

NORTHSOUTH
BOOKS

New York / London

Even as a calf, Gloria the Cow had been bigger than all the other calves. The older she got, the bigger she became. She had huge clunking hooves, thick legs, shaggy fur, and a fat stomach. Her head was as big as a pumpkin.

Despite this, Gloria dreamed of being a performer. And even though she walked as loopy as a camel and her voice was as gravelly as a cement mixer, in her heart, Gloria knew that she was no ordinary cow—she was destined to be a star!

Gloria desperately wanted to stand out from the rest of the herd. She couldn't change her hooves, her legs, her fur, or her face. But she could still change her appearance—she could start wearing clothes. Who wouldn't notice a cow wearing clothes? Of course, there were no clothes in her size. So Gloria had to sew everything herself. The results were mixed. Pants were especially difficult—she was always splitting them in the rear. But her clothes sure made her stand out!

Gloria was not interested in settling down and becoming an ordinary milk cow like the other cows her age. No, she was ambitious.

The fox, who was always teasing her, told Gloria that her voice was so beautiful she should train to be a singer. So she decided to do just that. She practiced for days until she was ready for her first big concert.

Lots of cows came to hear Gloria sing. Her first song was "Tiptoe Through the Tulips." Unfortunately, it was also her last song. For if her speaking voice sounded like a cement mixer, her singing voice sounded like a chain saw cutting through steel.

The audience covered their ears. When that didn't stop the noise, they whistled, screamed, and stomped as loudly as they could so they no longer heard Gloria's horrible singing. When that didn't work, they stampeded away.

Poor Gloria stopped singing and began to cry.

The other cows thought that perhaps now Gloria would settle down and become a good milk cow like everyone else.

But Gloria refused to give up. She decided to try her luck as a dancer and signed up for dance lessons the very next day.

The whole herd came to her first dance recital. Gloria clomped onto the stage in a homemade tutu she had cleverly fashioned from seven tablecloths.

Silence fell over the audience as the music began. Gloria took her position. She took a deep breath and began her dance. That's when she stumbled and tripped over her hooves.

The cows in the audience laughed, but Gloria would not be deterred.
She bravely continued to dance and leap.

But just as she completed a difficult grand jeté, the boards of the stage collapsed under her weight, and with them went Gloria.

The audience laughed and laughed.

Luckily, five strong oxen climbed onto the stage and helped her from the hole. Refusing to quit, in true diva fashion, she kept right on dancing.

Unfortunately, as she avoided the large hole in the stage, she accidentally pirouetted right off and crashed down on top of the musicians who had been accompanying her.

The bass broke, the trumpet smashed, the drum burst, the accordion was ripped in two. The band members looked at one another in astonishment. Then everyone started shouting. Except the conductor. He had swallowed his baton.

The audience roared with laughter as Gloria disappeared behind the curtain.

"Maybe now Gloria will finally give up her crazy dreams and settle down," said the other cows.

But Gloria would not even think about it. She knew there was an audience somewhere who would appreciate her. She just had to find it. So Gloria decided to take her show on the road. Her first stop was the land of the hippos, where she met plenty of nice, plump hippopotamuses. They were huge. They were gigantic. They were humongous!

All night she sang and danced for the hippos. Compared to these portly animals, Gloria looked like a tiny jewel on stage. The hippos loved her.

The next day the *Hippo News* raved: "We were privileged to see Gloria the Diva sing and dance last night. Never before have we heard such a pure and light voice. Never have we heard such beautiful melodies. And when Gloria danced—or more accurately, floated—she was like a dainty fairy, and every hippo in the audience was enchanted by her grace and charm. We eagerly await the next performance by Gloria the Cow—Gloria the Star—Gloria the DIVA!"

At last, Gloria had found an audience that appreciated just how very special she was.